A PIG, A FOX, AND A BOX

430

For Chad, Christopher, Amanda,
Michael, Katie, and Gregory.
Fine siblings all—JF

PENGUIN WORKSHOP
An Imprint of Penguin Random House LLC, New York

Copyright © 2015 by Jonathan Fenske. All rights reserved. Previously published in 2015 by Penguin Young Readers. This paperback edition published in 2019 by Penguin Workshop, an imprint of Penguin Random House LLC, New York. PENGUIN and PENGUIN WORKSHOP are trademarks of Penguin Books Ltd, and the W colophon is a registered trademark of Penguin Random House LLC. Printed in the USA.

Visit us online at www.penguinrandomhouse.com.

Library of Congress Control Number: 2014044337

ISBN 9780593094648   10 9 8 7 6 5 4 3 2 1

A PIG, A FOX, AND A BOX

by Jonathan Fenske

Penguin Workshop

PART ONE

5

6

Oh, Pig, come here!
Oh, Pig, come see!

Did I just hear
Fox call for me?

9

Here I sit.
I sit on top.

1.

2.

3.

BOOM!

The box went *BOOM*!
And I went *PLOP*!

Hee-hee.
I think I broke the box.

The box is flat.

PART TWO

Help, help, big Pig!
Oh help!
Come see!

Did I just hear
Fox call for me?

I will lift the rocks. I will throw them far.
I am coming, Fox! Stay where you are!

That big, big pile of heavy rocks was on a wig, not on a fox.

Help, help, big Pig!
Oh help!
Come see!
There is a pile of rocks on me!

24

I will leave the wig.
I will leave the rocks.

This wig is flat.

PART THREE

Pig was here